# GOOD GUYS,

by Joanne Rocklin    illustrated by Nancy Carpenter

# BAD GUYS

Abrams Books for Young Readers • New York

Here comes a bad guy,
sniffly and slouchy.

Up at five
sleepy and grouchy.

Teeth are missing
(hates to brush)—
doesn't really matter
mostly eats mush.

Here comes a good guy
fresh from a shower.

Squeaky-clean,
smells like a flower.

Doesn't eat sugar,
loves vitamin A—
teeth are brushed
twelve times a day.

Here come more bad guys
wearing pirate clothes—
patches on their eyes,
warts on their toes.

First to steal the treasure
dances to the bank.

Last one to burp
has to walk the plank.

But here come some good guys!
Great swimmers all.

High dives, backstroke,
Australian crawl.

Save your life
and won't let you drown
if you have to walk a plank
or your ship goes down.

Here come the bad guys,
green and scary—
smelly, yucky,
slimy, hairy.

Earth's more fun
than outer space,
so scare away
the human race!

But here come the good guys
wearing fancy capes.

Don't even try it—
nobody escapes.

Superguys come swooping
*ZIP! ZAP! ZOOM!*

They'll grab your slimy neck
and fly you to the moon.

Now come the bad guys
tickling piggy's ears.

Snatching all the hens' eggs,
rustling all the steers.

Eating ham and omelets,
gooey sugar pies,
*YEE-HAW-HAW!*-ing
till the wild wolf cries.

But here come the good guys—
*WOO-WOO-WOO!*

Capture your hearts
with a song or two.

Tame you all
with an awesome story,
but they'll only share the ending
when you say you're sorry.

Goodbye, all you great guys!

Time-out for bed.

"My turn to be a good guy!"
says a sleepyhead.

"OK," says a good guy.
"Tomorrow we'll switch."

Lights out.
Can't tell

which is which.

*For all my good guys and bad guys,
one and the same, with love*
*—J.R.*

*For my backyard buddies Shabnam and Robin*
*—N.C.*

The illustrations in this book were made with charcoal, watercolor, and digital media.

Cataloging-in-Publication Data has been applied for and may be obtained from the Library of Congress.

ISBN 978-1-4197-3417-5

Text copyright © 2020 Joanne Rocklin
Illustrations copyright © 2020 Nancy Carpenter
Book design by Steph Stilwell

Printed and bound in China
10 9 8 7 6 5 4 3 2 1

Abrams Books for Young Readers are available at special discounts when purchased in
quantity for premiums and promotions as well as fundraising or educational use.
Special editions can also be created to specification. For details, contact
specialsales@abramsbooks.com or the address below.

Abrams® is a registered trademark of Harry N. Abrams, Inc.

**ABRAMS** The Art of Books
195 Broadway, New York, NY 10007
abramsbooks.com